ORGANIC

Local

MENU

For my favorite food truck fest companions —A.P.

For Mom, the best chef I know. And Dad, for telling me to eat every last bite —M.D.

Farrar Straus Giroux Books for Young Readers
An imprint of Macmillan Publishing Group, LLC
175 Fifth Avenue, New York, NY 10010

Color separations by Bright Arts (H.K.) Ltd.
Printed in China by RR Donnelley Asia Printing Solutions Ltd.,
Dongguan City, Guangdong Province
Designed by Kristie Radwilowicz
First edition, 2018
10   9   8   7   6   5   4   3   2   1

mackids.com

Library of Congress Cataloging-in-Publication Data

Names: Penfold, Alexandra, author. | Dutton, Mike, illustrator.
Title: Food truck fest! / Alexandra Penfold ; pictures by Mike Dutton.
Description: First edition. | New York : Farrar Straus Giroux, 2018. |
  Summary: A family prepares for a day at the food truck festival, while at
  the same time, the food truck crews get ready for the same event, checking
  recipes, starting to cook, and driving to the festival site.
Identifiers: LCCN 2017010992 | ISBN 9780374303181 (hardcover)
Subjects: | CYAC: Stories in rhyme. | Food trucks—Fiction. |
  Festivals—Fiction.
Classification: LCC PZ8.3.P376 Fo 2018 | DDC [E]—dc23
LC record available at https://lccn.loc.gov/2017010992

Our books may be purchased in bulk for promotional, educational, or business use.
Please contact your local bookseller or the Macmillan Corporate and Premium Sales Department
at (800) 221-7945 ext. 5442 or by e-mail at MacmillanSpecialMarkets@macmillan.com.

FOOD TRUCK FEST!

ALEXANDRA PENFOLD   *Pictures by* **MIKE DUTTON**

Farrar Straus Giroux

New York

Over at the depot and up with the sun,
the food trucks get ready. Today will be fun!

Time to hustle, there's prep work to do.
Bring in the groceries. Here comes the crew.

Let's get moving, no time to rest.
Everybody's going to the food truck fest!

Family's up. It's a hullabaloo.
First, get dressed. Where's baby's shoe?

The sky is clear. The weather's great.
The lines get long. We can't be late!

Let's get moving, no time to rest.
Everybody's going to the food truck fest!

Check the recipe, start to cook.
Peek inside for a closer look.

Some trucks
have ovens,
others have grills.

They're kitchens
on wheels,
without the frills.

Each cook has a special job
preparing for the hungry mob . . .

Washing and drying.

Mincing and slicing.

Mixing and stirring.

He's making icing!

Let's get moving, no time to rest.
Everybody's going to the food truck fest!

Blanket, bug spray, sunblock, too.
Bags are packed, but where's that shoe?

Let's get moving, no time to rest.
Everybody's going to the food truck fest!

Engines rumble, then start to roar.
Close the windows, shut the door.

Ready and loaded with tons of good eats,
the fleet of mighty food trucks takes to the streets.

Uh-oh, blocked bridge! What can the trucks do?
The festival's today. They need to get through.

If they can't drive across, then they'll have to float.
Hurry up, drive aboard the big ferryboat.

The ferry is fast,
the trip will be quick.
The river is rough,
but trucks don't get sick.

Hold the ferry! Wait, wait, wait!
Four more passengers run through the gate.

Let's get moving, no time to rest.
Everybody's going to the food truck fest!

The caravan arrives—along with a crowd
that's excited, and eager, and rowdy, and loud.

Let's get moving, no time to rest.
Everybody's HUNGRY at the food truck fest!

The cooks get to work serving up lunch.
The lines may be long, but there are samples to munch.

Taste this morsel called falafel.

Or polish off a Belgian waffle.

Kimchi tacos,
that's no illusion.
Korean and Mexican
make a tasty fusion.

Folks settle down with their hot dogs and ices,
burritos, kebabs, pretzels, and slices.

A band's playing tunes and everyone's eating.
With such tasty food, who really needs seating?

Before too long, it's time for dessert.
Will you choose ice cream or frozen yogurt?

Soon the trucks serve up
their very last snack.
It's time to pack up,
they're all going back.

Home to the depot while it's still light,
to scrub and clean up . . .

Sweet dreams, good night!